MW00911416

BIRTHDAY

SNOW

Written by

Kim Messinger and Michael LaLumiere

Illustrated by Angela Ursillo

Stagger Lee Books

San Francisco

www.staggerleebooks.com

Copyright 2005 Michael LaLumiere and Kim Messinger

ISBN-13 978-0-9791006-1-1 ISBN-10 0-9791006-1-5

Dedicated

to the memory of

Francis J. LaLumiere

❄ Daniel's Tips On How To Make It Snow ❄

❄ Wear your pajamas inside out.

❄ Put four ice cubes in your toilet – but DO NOT flush until cubes have melted.

❄ Buy lots and lots of cocoa, marshmallows and milk.

❄ Do a snow dance with your mother.

❄ Put a snow yardstick by the door.

$\mathcal{D}$aniel was uncommonly patient for a boy with spiky red hair and freckles spattered across his nose. He looked out the window and studied the morning sky for signs of snow. It was his birthday and it always snowed on his birthday.

Daniel loved snow. When it snowed he got to wear shiny snow pants that whooshed when he walked. His mother made ice cream from big bowls of snow he scooped up from the front yard. He would run outside and let snowflakes pile up on his face.

Best of all, he got to zoom down the hill next door on his snow tube.

Daniel's 1st ♥ Birthday ♥

Snow had fallen on every one of Daniel's birthdays. He didn't remember all those white birthdays, but there were pictures in his special birthday album, so he knew it was true.

After breakfast Daniel called the weather man six times.
Each time he listened carefully. The weather man talked fast and
used big words, but the little boy was certain he heard the word snow.
It was his birthday. Snow was on the way.

"Mom, can I go outside now and wait for the snow? Where are my boots?"

Daniel's mom smiled. She pulled the basket of snow clothes out of the hall closet. She zipped him into his shiny snow suit but let Daniel pull a cap down over his ears himself. Finally, Daniel stuck out his hands and his mom pulled waterproof mittens over his wiggling fingers.

Daniel hurried to the garage to get his snow tube. All the winter gear weighed him down. He looked like a duck with black boots waddling across the yard.

At the top of the little hill next door, Daniel shaded his
eyes the best he could with his big, floppy mitten. The sun was
so bright he couldn't tell if there was a blizzard coming or not.

Two boys from down the street played catch with a football as they slowly made their way toward the park.

"Hey Daniel, what are you doing?" they called.

The little boy tugged his scarf down off his mouth so he could answer. "I'm waiting for snow."

The older boys laughed. "What snow? There aren't even any clouds."

"Snow is coming. The weather man on the phone said so."

"Boy, you don't know much about snow, do you? It doesn't matter what anyone on the phone says. Did you put four ice cubes in the toilet last night?"

"No."

"Did you wear your pajamas inside out?"

"No."

"Well, that's what you do to make sure it snows. You won't get a single flake if you don't put ice cubes in the toilet or wear your pajamas inside out."

The two boys laughed again. Daniel wondered why no one had told him about the ice cubes and pajamas.

Daniel sighed when he saw his big sister, Caitlin, striding toward him. Maybe if he kept staring at the sky and didn't say anything, she would go away.

"Why are you standing out here in your snow clothes, Daniel? If it was going to snow Mom would be doing her SNOW things."

"Did she go to the grocery store and buy a cart full of cocoa, marshmallows, and gallons of milk for snow ice cream? NO!"

"Did she put a yardstick by the front door so we can measure how deep the snow is every ten minutes? Keep your eye on Mom, Daniel. You can't expect snow if Mom isn't doing her SNOW things."

Daniel watched his sister stomp away. For a moment he felt worried. But only for a moment. It was his birthday. Snow was on the way.

At noon, Daniel's mother carried a picnic lunch up the little hill.

"Hey, Birthday Boy! Are you hungry? I think it would be all right if you sat on your snow tube to rest and eat a little. You don't have to take off your mittens. Just open wide."

Piece by piece, Daniel's mother fed him a sandwich made with peanut butter and red raspberry preserves. Daniel was happy that she had cut off the crusts, although he wouldn't have complained if she had forgotten. For dessert there was a cinnamony snickerdoodle.

After swallowing his last bite, Daniel said, "You haven't been doing your snow things, Mom. Don't you think it will snow?"

His mom looked up into the bright sun. "It's your birthday, Daniel. It has always snowed on your birthday. I guess we'll have to wait and see."

"It might help if you got ready like you usually do, Mom. Maybe you could make some hot chocolate and put the yard stick by the door."

Daniel searched the sky for any clouds that might have snuck up while he was eating. "Thanks for the lunch, Mom. I'm going to stay here and keep waiting for the snow, okay?"

"Good idea, Daniel. But be careful when the blizzard hits," said his mom.

An hour went by and it seemed to Daniel that the sky was getting bluer. The mail man stopped his truck at the curb. "Hey Daniel, how are you?"

"Hello Mr. Peterson. I've been waiting for snow all day, and I'm getting tired. You drive all over the place, right? Have you seen any snow today?"

"Can't say that I have, Daniel. Maybe it will snow tomorrow."

"It's my birthday TODAY. It always snows on my birthday. I'm going to be the first to slide down this hill."

"Well, Happy Birthday, Daniel! Did you remember to put ice cubes in your toilet last night?"

Daniel looked down at his boots. "No. I didn't know."

"Try it next year. It might help."

Daniel waited
another hour and then
trudged home. His mother
was waiting at the door.
"C'mon Daniel, let's get those
snow clothes off. I think I know
what's been missing. We need to do
a snow dance! I can't believe I didn't
think of it sooner!"

In the family room, Daniel's Mom put a CD in the player.
"Are you ready Daniel?"
"Yes, Mom, I'm ready. But I don't know all the words."
"Don't worry about singing, Daniel. This is a snow DANCE!"
Daniel and his Mom held hands and twirled around the room.
Once, Daniel's mom spun him in a circle. He felt dizzy but
hoped she would do it again.

When the song ended, Daniel wrapped his arms around his mom's legs. "Thanks, Mom. It'll snow now for sure. While we wait, can we look at my birthday pictures?"

Daniel snuggled against his mom while she turned the pages of his special birthday album and described each photograph.

"That's you, Daniel, just a few hours old. See Dad outside the window, building your first snowman? . . . This picture is from last year. Look how deep the snow is. Caitlin showed you how to make a snow angel. When you tried it yourself, you got stuck. Do you remember?"

Daniel didn't answer. He was sound asleep.

Daniel dreamed of whooshing down a snowy mountain on his inner tube, his scarf flapping as he zoomed by hundreds of penguins and polar bears. At the bottom of the mountain he heard a loud voice calling him. Someone shook his arm.

"Wake up, Daniel! Wake up!" said Caitlin.

Daniel covered his eyes. "I don't want to wake up. I'm having a snow dream."

His mom laughed. "You can keep your eyes closed. We have a surprise for you!"

Daniel kept his eyes shut tight while Caitlin and his mom led him to the big window at the front of the house.

Finally, his mom said, "Open your eyes, Daniel."

When he did, Daniel saw big flakes of birthday snow drifting softly to the ground. The roads, the grass and the little hill next door were already white.

They put on their snow clothes and went outside. At the top of the hill, Daniel's mom leaned close to her son's ear and whispered, "Daniel, it may not always snow on your birthday but you should always believe it will. And if you run into trouble we can always do our special dance. Okay?"

And then she gave the tube a little push that sent Daniel whooshing down the snowy hill.